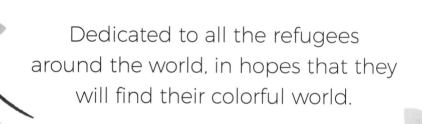

Dedicated to all the refugees
around the world, in hopes that they
will find their colorful world.

THE BLUE SCARF

Written by
MOHAMED DANAWI

Illustrated by
RUAIDA MANNAA

RP|KIDS
PHILADELPHIA

Layla lives in the world of Blue.

She loves her warm and peaceful world.

On her birthday, her mother gives her a blue silk scarf,
which she loves dearly and often wears
around her neck.

But one early spring morning, a heavy rain of fire
starts falling from the dark blue sky.

As Layla rushes for shelter, the violent storm blows her scarf off her neck, carrying the scarf high into the air.

Layla chases after her precious gift,
but it vanishes into the dark clouds.

With fire still raining down from the sky,
Layla runs to the shore and hops in her blue boat.

Scared but determined, she sets sail into
the vast ocean, in search of her beloved scarf.

Layla sails night and day, until her boat docks in a strange new world of Green.

She calls out in despair, "Hello, Green world, have you seen my blue scarf?" An answer echoes from the crowd at the shore: "We have not seen anything blue here. You will need to look for it in another world."

The wind takes Layla and her boat to the world of Yellow—
a sandy world with giant monuments.

But when Layla asks about her
blue scarf, she receives the same answer.

She searches for her blue scarf
in the world of Red...

and in the world of Orange...

and even in the world of Purple...

but no one has seen her blue scarf.

After a long journey through the sea, Layla's boat arrives at a world beaming with a rainbow of colors, a mosaic of shapes, and plentiful aromas, all beautifully woven together in one land. It is unlike anything Layla has seen or experienced.

Layla calls out one final time:
"Hello, Rainbow world, have you seen my blue scarf?"
And the people of the Rainbow world point above
her, saying, "Look up! On the tip of the boat's mast.
Is that what you are looking for?"

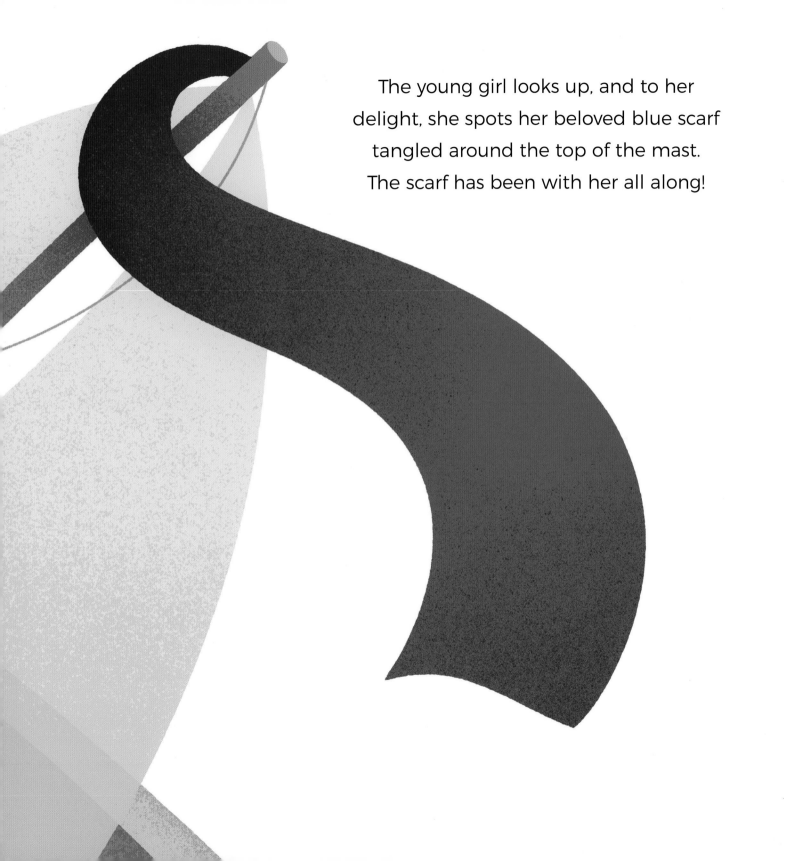

The young girl looks up, and to her delight, she spots her beloved blue scarf tangled around the top of the mast. The scarf has been with her all along!

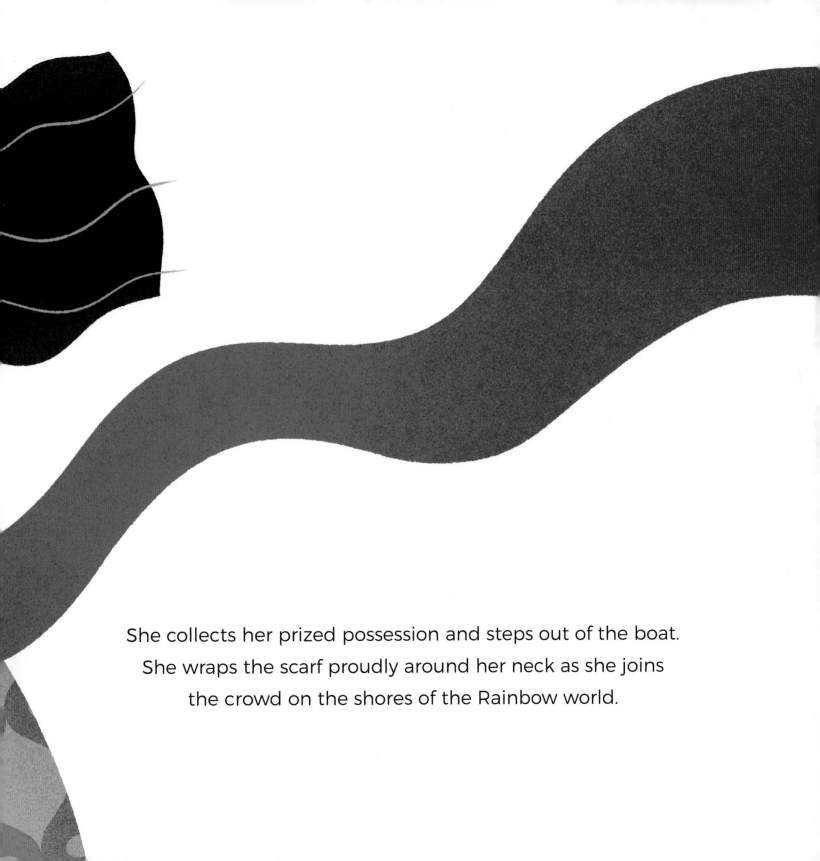

She collects her prized possession and steps out of the boat.
She wraps the scarf proudly around her neck as she joins
the crowd on the shores of the Rainbow world.

The people welcome and embrace Layla. She smiles for she has found a new world—a world of blue, green, yellow, orange, red, and purple.

The colors of this world are beautifully intertwined, and the
people are loving, welcoming, and generous.
Layla continues to wear her blue scarf, day in and
day out, proudly around her neck.

Like Layla, know that your scarf is your identity. Proudly wear
who you are no matter where you are. And if you ever think
you've lost it, remember that it will never truly leave you, no matter
where you go or what new and colorful world you join.

Running Press Kids
Hachette Book Group
1290 Avenue of the Americas, New York, NY 10104
www.runningpress.com/rpkids
@RP_Kids

Printed in China

First Edition: October 2022

Published by Running Press Kids, an imprint of Perseus Books, LLC, a subsidiary of Hachette Book Group, Inc. The Running Press Kids name and logo is a trademark of the Hachette Book Group.

The Hachette Speakers Bureau provides a wide range of authors for speaking events. To find out more, go to www.hachettespeakersbureau.com or call (866) 376-6591.

The publisher is not responsible for websites (or their content) that are not owned by the publisher.

Print book cover and interior design by Frances J. Soo Ping Chow.

Library of Congress Cataloging-in-Publication Data
Names: Danawi, Mohamed, author. | Mannaa, Ruaida, illustrator. Title: The blue scarf / written by Mohamed Danawi; illustrated by Ruaida Mannaa. Description: First edition. | New York, NY : Running Press Kids, 2022. | Audience: Ages 4-8. | Summary: When she loses her beloved scarf, Layla becomes a refugee from her Blue world, journeying to worlds of different colors and searching for her prized possession. Identifiers: LCCN 2021013892 (print) | LCCN 2021013893 (ebook) | ISBN 9780762478897 (hardcover) | ISBN 9780762478903 (ebook) Subjects: CYAC: Refugees—Fiction. | Color—Fiction. | Voyages and travels—Fiction. | LCGFT: Picture books. Classification: LCC PZ7.1.D296 Bl 2022 (print) | LCC PZ7.1.D296 (ebook) | DDC [E]—dc23 LC record available at https://lccn.loc.gov/2021013892 LC ebook record available at https://lccn.loc.gov/2021013893

ISBNs: 978-0-7624-7889-7 (hardcover), 978-0-7624-7890-3 (ebook), 978-0-7624-8014-2 (ebook), 978-0-7624-8015-9 (ebook)

1010

10 9 8 7 6 5 4 3 2 1